Biscuit magic

pil

Publications International, Ltd.

All recipes that contain specific brand names are copyrighted by those companies and/or associations, unless otherwise specified. Photo on page 68 © Veg•All®; photo on page 85 © Watkins Incorporated. All other photographs © 2010 Publications International, Ltd.

Some of the products listed in this publication may be in limited distribution.

Pictured on the front cover (clockwise from top left): Chocolate Chip Cherry Biscuits *(page 76),* Savory Veg•All® Steak Pot Pie *(page 38),* Omelet Biscuits *(page 16),* and Sausage Pinwheels *(page 28).*

ISBN-13: 978-1-4508-1721-9
ISBN-10: 1-4508-1721-1

Manufactured in China.

8 7 6 5 4 3 2 1

Microwave Cooking: Microwave ovens vary in wattage. Use the cooking times as guidelines and check for doneness before adding more time.

Contents

breakfast, brunch and beyond

Biscuit and Sausage Bake

- **2 cups biscuit baking mix**
- **½ cup milk**
- **1 egg**
- **1 teaspoon vanilla**
- **1 cup fresh or frozen blueberries**
- **6 fully cooked breakfast sausage links, thawed if frozen**
- **Warm maple syrup**

1. Preheat oven to 350°F. Coat 8-inch square baking pan with nonstick cooking spray.

2. Combine biscuit mix, milk, egg and vanilla in medium bowl. Gently fold in blueberries. (Batter will be stiff.) Spread batter in prepared pan. Cut each sausage link into small pieces; sprinkle over batter.

3. Bake 22 minutes or until top is lightly browned. Cut into squares; serve with maple syrup.

Makes 6 servings

Sawmill Biscuits and Gravy

GRAVY

3	**tablespoons canola or vegetable oil, divided**
8	**ounces regular or reduced-fat bulk breakfast sausage**
3	**tablespoons biscuit baking mix**
2	**cups whole milk**
¼	**teaspoon salt, or to taste**
¼	**teaspoon black pepper, or to taste**

BISCUITS

2¼	**cups biscuit baking mix**
⅔	**cup whole milk**

1. Preheat oven to 450°F. Heat 1 tablespoon oil in large nonstick skillet over medium heat until hot. Add sausage; cook and stir until browned, breaking up larger pieces. Remove with slotted spoon; set aside.

2. Add remaining 2 tablespoons oil to skillet. Add 3 tablespoons biscuit mix; whisk until smooth. Gradually stir in 2 cups milk; cook and stir 3 to 4 minutes or until mixture comes to a boil. Cook 1 minute, stirring constantly. Stir in sausage and any juices. Cook and stir 2 minutes. Add salt and pepper.

3. Combine 2¼ cups biscuit mix and ⅔ cup milk. Spoon 8 mounds onto ungreased nonstick baking sheet. Bake 8 to 10 minutes or until golden. Serve warm with gravy.

Makes 8 servings

Chorizo and Cheddar Breakfast Casserole

- 8 **ounces chorizo sausage, removed from casing**
- 1 **cup diced onion**
- 1 **medium green bell pepper, chopped**
- 1 **jalapeño pepper,* chopped**
- 6 **large eggs, beaten**
- ¾ **cup biscuit baking mix**
- ⅔ **cup buttermilk****
- ½ **teaspoon salt**
- ½ **teaspoon black pepper**
- 1 **cup (4 ounces) shredded Mexican cheese blend or Monterey Jack with hot peppers**
- ¼ **cup chopped fresh cilantro**
- ½ **cup sour cream**
  Chopped tomato (optional)

*Jalapeño peppers can sting and irritate the skin, so wear rubber gloves when handling, and do not touch your eyes.

**If you don't have buttermilk, substitute 2 teaspoons vinegar or lemon juice plus enough milk to equal ⅔ cup. Let stand 5 minutes.

1. Preheat oven to 350°F. Coat 11×7-inch baking pan or 9-inch deep-dish pie pan with nonstick cooking spray; set aside.

2. Heat medium ovenproof nonstick skillet over medium heat until hot. Add chorizo; cook and stir 4 minutes or until browned, breaking up large pieces. Add onion, bell pepper and jalapeño; cook and stir 6 minutes or until crisp-tender. Transfer to prepared baking pan.

3. Combine eggs, biscuit mix, buttermilk, salt and black pepper in medium bowl; mix well. Pour over sausage mixture in baking pan.

4. Bake, uncovered, 30 minutes or until knife inserted comes out clean. Remove from oven. Sprinkle evenly with cheese and cilantro. Let stand 10 minutes before serving with sour cream and tomato, if desired.

Makes 6 servings

Peach Pecan Upside-Down Pancake

- **2   tablespoons butter, melted**
- **2   tablespoons packed light brown sugar**
- **1   tablespoon maple syrup**
- **½   (16-ounce) package frozen unsweetened peach slices, thawed**
- **3   tablespoons pecan pieces**
- **⅔   cup biscuit baking mix**
- **2   eggs**
- **⅓   cup fat-free (skim) milk**
- **½   teaspoon vanilla**
- **Additional maple syrup (optional)**

1. Preheat oven to 400°F. Coat 8- or 9-inch pie pan with nonstick cooking spray.

2. Pour butter into pie pan. Sprinkle with brown sugar and maple syrup. Arrange peach slices in single layer on top in decorative circle. Sprinkle with pecans.

3. Place biscuit mix in medium bowl. Whisk eggs, milk and vanilla in small bowl; stir into biscuit mix just until dry ingredients are moistened. Pour batter over peaches.

4. Bake 15 to 18 minutes or until lightly browned and toothpick inserted into center comes out clean. Cool 1 minute. Run knife around outer edge of pan. Invert onto serving plate. Serve immediately with additional maple syrup, if desired.

Makes 6 servings

Better Blueberry Scones

- **3   cups reduced-fat biscuit baking mix**
- **¾   cup whole-wheat pastry flour**
- **¼   cup canola or vegetable oil**
- **3   tablespoons packed brown sugar**
- **¾   cup fresh blueberries**
- **½   cup plain fat-free yogurt**
- **½   cup fat-free (skim) milk**
- **1   to 2 teaspoons cinnamon-sugar (optional)**

1. Preheat oven to 400°F. Lightly coat baking sheet with nonstick cooking spray.

2. Combine biscuit mix and flour in large bowl. Cut in oil with pastry cutter or two knives until mixture resembles coarse crumbs. Add sugar and blueberries; mix lightly.

3. Blend yogurt and milk in small bowl. Add to flour mixture, stirring lightly only until blended and soft dough forms. (Do not overmix.) Add more milk, 1 tablespoon at a time, if necessary.

4. With floured hands, pat dough into round 1½ inches thick. Score into 16 wedges. If desired, sprinkle with cinnamon-sugar.

5. Bake 10 to 12 minutes. Remove from oven and cut apart on score lines. Bake 2 to 4 minutes longer or until golden brown and toothpick inserted in center comes out clean.

Makes 16 scones

Cranberry Orange Coffee Cake

- 1½ **cups biscuit baking mix**
- ⅓ **cup granulated sugar**
- ⅓ **cup sour cream**
- 1 **egg**
- 1 **teaspoon vanilla**
- 2 **tablespoons orange juice**
- 1 **tablespoon plus 1 teaspoon grated orange peel, divided**
- 1 **cup fresh or frozen whole cranberries**
- ½ **cup chopped dried fruit (such as apricots or golden raisins)***
- ⅓ **cup coarsely chopped walnuts**
- ½ **cup packed brown sugar**
- 2 **tablespoons butter, softened**
- **Whipped cream (optional)**

*Lightly coat knife with nonstick cooking spray to prevent sticking.

1. Preheat oven to 350°F. Coat 12-inch tart pan with removable bottom with nonstick cooking spray; set aside.

2. Combine biscuit mix and granulated sugar in large bowl. Combine sour cream, egg, vanilla, orange juice and 1 tablespoon orange peel in medium bowl; beat well. Add to dry ingredients; stir until just moistened. Spread into prepared tart pan.

3. Sprinkle cranberries, dried fruit and walnuts over batter. Combine brown sugar, butter and remaining 1 teaspoon orange peel in small bowl; mix well. Sprinkle evenly over fruit.

4. Bake 25 to 30 minutes or until lightly browned. Serve warm with whipped cream, if desired.

Makes 12 servings

Omelet Biscuits

- **1 container (about 16 ounces) large refrigerated flaky biscuits (8 biscuits)**
- **8 tablespoons tomato sauce**
- **2 slices turkey bacon**
- **¼ cup chopped onion**
- **¼ cup chopped green bell pepper**
- **1¼ cups cholesterol-free egg substitute**
- **¼ teaspoon black pepper**
- **½ cup (2 ounces) shredded reduced-fat Cheddar cheese**

1. Preheat oven to 375°F. Place biscuits 2 inches apart on large ungreased baking sheet. Make indentation in center of each biscuit. Spoon 1 tablespoon tomato sauce into center.

2. Cook bacon in large nonstick skillet over medium-high heat until crisp. Transfer to paper towels. Add onion and bell pepper to skillet. Cook and stir 2 to 3 minutes or until onion is translucent; set aside.

3. Coat same skillet with nonstick cooking spray. Pour in egg substitute; season with black pepper. Cook and stir 1 minute or until set.

4. Spoon eggs evenly into biscuit centers. Crumble bacon and mix into vegetables; sprinkle mixture evenly over eggs. Top with cheese. Bake 15 to 17 minutes or until biscuit edges are golden brown.

Makes 8 servings

Variation: Substitute low-fat sausage for the bacon, or try another of your favorite cheeses instead of Cheddar.

Whip 'em Up Wacky Waffles

  1½ **cups biscuit baking mix**
   1 **cup buttermilk**
   1 **large egg**
   1 **tablespoon vegetable oil**
  ½ **cup "M&M's"® Semi-Sweet Chocolate Mini Baking Bits**
      Powdered sugar and maple syrup

Preheat Belgian waffle iron. In large bowl, combine baking mix, buttermilk, egg and oil until well mixed. Spoon about ½ cup batter into hot waffle iron. Sprinkle with about 2 tablespoons "M&M's"® Semi-Sweet Chocolate Mini Baking Bits; top with about ½ cup batter. Close lid and bake until steaming stops, 1 to 2 minutes.* Sprinkle with powdered sugar and serve immediately with maple syrup and additional "M&M's"® Semi-Sweet Chocolate Mini Baking Bits.

Makes 4 Belgian waffles

*Check the manufacturer's directions for recommended amount of batter and baking time.

Chocolate Waffles: Substitute 1¼ cups biscuit baking mix, ¼ cup unsweetened cocoa powder and ½ cup sugar for biscuit baking mix. Prepare and cook as directed above.

Tip: These waffles make a great dessert too! Serve them with a scoop of ice cream, chocolate sauce and a sprinkle of "M&M's"® Chocolate Mini Baking Bits.

Apple and Cheese Pockets

2   cups Golden Delicious apples, peeled, cored and finely chopped (about 2 medium)

2   cups (8 ounces) shredded sharp Cheddar cheese

2   tablespoons apple jelly

¼   teaspoon curry powder

1   container (about 16 ounces) large reduced-fat refrigerated biscuits (8 biscuits)

1. Preheat oven to 350°F. Line baking sheet with parchment paper; set aside.

2. Combine apples, cheese, jelly and curry powder in large bowl; stir well.

3. Roll out biscuit on lightly floured surface to 6½-inch circle. Place ½ cup apple mixture in center. Fold biscuit over filling to form semicircle; press to seal tightly. Place on baking sheet. Repeat with remaining biscuits and filling.

4. Bake 15 to 18 minutes or until biscuits are golden and filling is heated through.

Makes 8 servings

Note: Refrigerate leftovers up to 2 days or freeze up to 1 month. To reheat thawed pockets, place in microwave oven about 30 seconds on HIGH (100% power) or until heated through.

Easy Pineapple Buns

⅔ **cup packed brown sugar**

¼ **cup maple syrup**

2 **tablespoons butter, melted**

1 **teaspoon vanilla**

1 **can (8 ounces) pineapple tidbits, drained**

½ **cup chopped pecans**

½ **cup flaked coconut**

1 **container (about 12 ounces) refrigerated flaky biscuits (10 biscuits)**

1. Preheat oven to 350°F.

2. Combine brown sugar, maple syrup, butter and vanilla in 11×7-inch baking dish. Sprinkle with pineapple tidbits, pecans and coconut.

3. Cut biscuits into quarters; arrange over coconut. Bake 25 to 30 minutes or until deep golden brown. Invert onto serving plate; serve warm.

Makes 10 servings

Cherry Scones with Buttery Fruit Spread

SCONES

- 2 **cups reduced-fat biscuit baking mix**
- 2 **tablespoons sugar**
- 1 **teaspoon grated lemon peel**
- ⅓ **cup fat-free (skim) milk**
- ¼ **cup dried cherries or dried cherries mixed with golden raisins**
- 1 **large egg, separated**
- 1 **teaspoon water**

FRUIT SPREAD

- ½ **cup diet margarine**
- ¼ **cup strawberry fruit spread**
- ½ **teaspoon vanilla**

1. Preheat oven to 400°F. Coat nonstick baking sheet with nonstick cooking spray.

2. Combine biscuit mix, sugar, lemon peel, milk, cherries and egg yolk in medium bowl. Form dough into ball. Roll out to ½-inch thickness on floured work surface. Cut out scones with 2-inch biscuit cutter. Gather scraps and reroll as necessary. Place scones on baking sheet.

3. Whisk egg white and water in small bowl with fork until well blended. Brush evenly over scones. Bake 10 minutes.

4. Mix margarine, fruit spread and vanilla in small bowl with fork until well blended. Serve with scones.

Makes 12 scones

Breakfast Pizza

1   container (10 ounces) refrigerated biscuits (10 biscuits)
½   pound sliced bacon, cooked, crumbled
2   tablespoons butter
2   tablespoons all-purpose flour
¼   teaspoon salt
⅛   teaspoon black pepper
1½   cups milk
½   cup (2 ounces) shredded reduced-fat Cheddar cheese
¼   cup sliced green onions
¼   cup chopped red bell pepper

1. Preheat oven to 350°F. Coat 13×9-inch baking dish with nonstick cooking spray. Prepare bacon; set aside.

2. Separate biscuit dough; arrange in rectangle on lightly floured surface. Roll into 14×10-inch rectangle. Place in prepared dish; pat edges up sides of dish. Bake 15 minutes. Remove from oven; set aside.

3. Melt butter in medium saucepan over medium heat. Stir in flour, salt and black pepper until smooth. Gradually stir in milk; cook and stir until thickened. Stir in cheese until melted. Spread sauce evenly over baked crust. Arrange bacon, green onions and bell pepper over sauce.

4. Bake, uncovered, 20 minutes or until crust is golden brown.

Makes 6 servings

Peach Streusel Coffee Cake

2½ **cups biscuit baking mix, divided**

⅔ **cup milk**

1 **egg**

¼ **cup granulated sugar**

1 **teaspoon ground cinnamon**

1 **teaspoon vanilla**

1 **package (16 ounces) frozen unsweetened peaches, thawed and diced**

½ **cup packed dark brown sugar**

½ **cup pecan pieces**

3 **tablespoons cold butter, diced**

1. Preheat oven to 375°F. Coat 9-inch square baking pan with nonstick cooking spray.

2. Place 2 cups biscuit mix in medium bowl; break up any lumps with spoon. Add milk, egg, granulated sugar, cinnamon and vanilla; stir until well blended. Add peaches; stir just until blended. Pour batter into prepared pan.

3. Combine remaining ½ cup biscuit mix and brown sugar in small bowl; stir until well blended. Add pecans and butter; toss gently (do not break up small pieces of butter). Sprinkle evenly over batter.

4. Bake 35 minutes or until toothpick inserted into center comes out clean. Cool in pan on wire rack 15 minutes. Serve warm or at room temperature.

Makes 9 servings

appetizing bites

Herbed Cheese Twists

- **2 tablespoons butter or margarine**
- **¼ cup grated Parmesan cheese**
- **1 teaspoon dried parsley flakes**
- **1 teaspoon dried basil**
- **1 container (about 6 ounces) refrigerated buttermilk biscuits (5 biscuits)**

1. Preheat oven to 400°F. Line baking sheet with parchment paper or coat with nonstick cooking spray; set aside.

2. Microwave butter in small microwave-safe bowl on MEDIUM (50% power) just until melted; cool slightly. Stir in cheese, parsley and basil.

3. Pat each biscuit into 5×2-inch rectangle. Spread 1 teaspoon butter mixture onto each rectangle; cut each into 3 lengthwise strips. Twist each strip 3 or 4 times. Place on prepared baking sheet. Bake 8 to 10 minutes or until golden brown.

Makes 15 twists

Parmesan Sliders

¾ **to 1 cup freshly shredded Parmesan cheese**
⅓ **cup milk**
1¼ **teaspoons chili powder**
½ **teaspoon sugar**
1 **cup biscuit baking mix**
1 **tablespoon cold unsalted butter, cut in thin slices**
  Dijon-style mustard
  Thinly sliced prosciutto, deli pastrami or ham

1. Preheat oven to 400°F. Line baking sheet with parchment paper; set aside. Spread cheese on large plate; set aside. Combine milk, chili powder and sugar in small bowl. Stir well; set aside 5 minutes.

2. Place biscuit mix in medium bowl. Cut in butter with pastry blender or two knives until mixture resembles coarse crumbs. Add milk mixture; stir gently to form soft sticky dough. Drop dough by rounded tablespoonfuls onto cheese; gently roll dough to coat all sides with cheese. Place on prepared baking sheet.

3. Bake 13 to 14 minutes or until biscuits are golden. Transfer biscuits to wire rack to cool slightly. To serve, split each biscuit. Spread mustard on bottom half. Evenly divide prosciutto among biscuits and top with remaining halves.

Makes 10 to 12 appetizers

Sausage Pinwheels

2 cups biscuit mix
½ cup milk
¼ cup butter or margarine, melted
1 pound BOB EVANS® Original Recipe Roll Sausage

1. Combine biscuit mix, milk and butter in large bowl until blended. Refrigerate 30 minutes.

2. Divide dough into two portions. Roll out one portion on floured surface to ⅛-inch-thick rectangle, about 10×7 inches. Spread with half the sausage. Roll lengthwise into long roll. Repeat with remaining dough and sausage. Place rolls in freezer until firm enough to cut easily.

3. Preheat oven to 400°F. Cut rolls into thin slices. Place on ungreased baking sheets. Bake 15 minutes or until golden brown. Serve hot. Refrigerate leftovers.

Makes 48 pinwheels

Note: This recipe can be doubled. Refreeze after slicing. When ready to serve, thaw slices in refrigerator and bake.

Rosemary Parmesan Biscuit Poppers

- 2¼ **cups biscuit baking mix**
- ⅔ **cup milk**
- ⅓ **cup grated Parmesan cheese, divided**
- 1 **tablespoon chopped fresh rosemary or 1 teaspoon dried rosemary, crumbled**
- 1 **tablespoon grated lemon peel**
- ⅛ **teaspoon ground red pepper**
- 3 **tablespoons extra-virgin olive oil**
- ⅛ **to ¼ teaspoon salt**

1. Preheat oven to 450°F. Coat large nonstick baking sheet with nonstick cooking spray; set aside.

2. Combine biscuit mix, milk, ¼ cup cheese, rosemary, lemon peel and red pepper in medium bowl; mix until blended. Spoon by teaspoonfuls in 1-inch mounds onto prepared baking sheet; sprinkle evenly with remaining cheese.

3. Bake 8 to 10 minutes or until lightly golden. Remove from oven. Brush oil evenly over biscuits; sprinkle evenly with salt. Serve immediately.

Makes 24 appetizers

Spicy Lamb & Potato Nests

POTATO NESTS

- 2 unpeeled small Colorado potatoes, shredded
- 1 egg
- 1 tablespoon vegetable oil
- 1 tablespoon grated Parmesan cheese
- ¼ teaspoon garlic powder
- ¼ teaspoon black pepper
- ¼ cup biscuit mix
  Fine, dry bread crumbs

LAMB FILLING

- 8 ounces lean ground lamb
- ¼ cup chopped green onions
- 1 teaspoon grated fresh ginger or ¼ teaspoon dry ginger
- ½ teaspoon ground cumin
- ¼ teaspoon salt
- ¼ teaspoon ground coriander
- ¼ teaspoon ground cinnamon
- ¼ teaspoon ground red pepper
- ¼ cup jalapeño pepper jelly

1. To prepare Potato Nests, place shredded potatoes in medium bowl. Cover with cold water; let stand 5 minutes. Drain well; pat dry with paper towels. Preheat oven to 400°F.

2. Whisk together egg, oil, cheese, garlic powder and black pepper. Stir in biscuit mix until well blended. Stir in shredded potatoes. Generously grease 16 muffin cups; sprinkle bottom of each lightly with bread crumbs. Spoon about 1 tablespoon potato mixture into each cup; make slight indentation in center. Bake 15 minutes. Remove from oven and keep warm.

3. Meanwhile, to prepare Lamb Filling, cook and stir lamb and onions in saucepan over medium-high heat until lamb is no longer pink and onions are tender. Drain well; add ginger, cumin, salt, coriander, cinnamon and red pepper. Cook and stir 1 to 2 minutes until flavors are blended. Add jelly; heat until jelly is melted and lamb mixture is heated through. Spoon lamb mixture by rounded teaspoonfuls onto Potato Nests. Serve hot.

Makes 16 appetizers

Note: Spicy Lamb & Potato Nests may be made ahead, covered and refrigerated. Just before serving, wrap in foil, and heat in preheated 350°F oven for 10 minutes.

Favorite recipe from **Colorado Potato Administrative Committee**

Turkey Bacon Biscuits

**5 JENNIE-O TURKEY STORE® Turkey Bacon slices,
cooked, crumbled, divided**

1 (8-ounce) package cream cheese, softened

2 eggs

2 tablespoons milk

½ cup shredded Swiss cheese

2 tablespoons chopped green onion

1 (10-ounce) can refrigerated flaky biscuits

1. Heat oven to 375°F. Grease 10 muffin cups.

2. In small bowl, beat cream cheese, eggs and milk with electric mixer at low speed until smooth. Stir in Swiss cheese and green onion.

3. Separate dough into 10 biscuits. Place 1 biscuit in each greased muffin cup; firmly press in bottom and up sides, forming ¼-inch rim. Place half of bacon in bottom of dough-lined muffin cups. Spoon cheese mixture over bacon. Bake 20 to 25 minutes or until filling is set and biscuits are golden brown.

4. Sprinkle each cup with remaining bacon; lightly press into filling. Remove from pan.

Makes 10 servings

Punched Pizza Rounds

1	container (12 ounces) refrigerated flaky buttermilk biscuits (10 biscuits)
80	mini pepperoni slices or 20 small pepperoni slices
8 to 10	pickled jalapeño slices, chopped (optional)
1	tablespoon dried basil, crushed
½	cup pizza sauce
1½	cups (6 ounces) shredded mozzarella
	Shredded Parmesan cheese (optional)

1. Preheat oven to 400°F. Coat 20 standard (2½-inch) nonstick muffin cups with nonstick cooking spray; set aside.

2. Split each biscuit in half, creating 20 rounds. Place in prepared muffin cups. Press 4 mini pepperoni slices into center of each round. Sprinkle evenly with jalapeños, if desired, and basil. Spread pizza sauce evenly into rounds. Sprinkle evenly with mozzarella cheese.

3. Bake 8 to 9 minutes or until golden on bottom. Remove from oven. Sprinkle evenly with Parmesan cheese, if desired. Remove from muffin cups after 1 to 2 minutes to prevent sticking. Serve warm.

Makes 20 appetizers

Easy Empanadas

1   cup prepared refrigerated barbecued shredded pork
2   tablespoons ORTEGA® Taco Sauce
1   tablespoon ORTEGA® Fire-Roasted Diced Green Chiles
1   can (12 count) refrigerated biscuits
1   egg, well beaten
1   cup ORTEGA® Black Bean & Corn Salsa

1. Preheat oven to 375°F. Mix pork, taco sauce and chiles in small bowl.

2. Separate biscuits into 12 pieces. Flatten each biscuit into 6-inch round, using rolling pin. Divide filling evenly among biscuits, spreading over half of each round to within ¼ inch of edge. Fold dough over filling; press edges with fork to seal well. Place on ungreased cookie sheet.

3. Brush tops with beaten egg. Bake 12 to 15 minutes or until edges are golden brown. Immediately remove from cookie sheet. Serve warm with salsa for dipping.

Makes 12 empanadas

Cheese Surprise Bites

- ⅓ **cup milk**
- 1 **tablespoon dehydrated chives**
- 1 **teaspoon minced fresh dill weed**
- ½ **teaspoon sugar**
- 1 **cup biscuit baking mix**
- 1 **tablespoon cold unsalted butter, cut in thin slices**
- 12 **cubes (½ inch each) sharp Cheddar cheese, well chilled**

1. Preheat oven to 400°F. Line baking sheet with parchment paper; set aside. Combine milk, chives, dill and sugar in small bowl. Stir well; set aside 5 minutes.

2. Place biscuit mix in medium bowl. Cut in butter with pastry blender or two knives until mixture resembles coarse crumbs. Add milk mixture; stir gently to form soft sticky dough. Divide dough equally into 12 walnut-sized balls. Gently push 1 cheese cube into each ball and form dough around cube, sealing well. Place on prepared baking sheet.

3. Bake 12 to 14 minutes or until biscuits are golden. Transfer biscuits to wire rack to cool slightly. Serve hot or warm.

Makes 12 biscuits

main courses

Skillet Chicken Pot Pie

**1   can (10¾ ounces) fat-free reduced-sodium
      cream of chicken soup, undiluted**
1¼ cups fat-free (skim) milk, divided
1   package (10 ounces) frozen mixed vegetables
2   cups diced cooked chicken
½   teaspoon black pepper
1   cup buttermilk biscuit mix
¼   teaspoon dried summer savory or parsley (optional)

1. Heat soup, 1 cup milk, vegetables, chicken and pepper in medium skillet over medium heat until mixture comes to a boil.

2. Combine biscuit mix and summer savory, if desired, in small bowl. Stir in remaining 3 to 4 tablespoons milk just until soft batter is formed. Drop batter by tablespoonfuls onto chicken mixture to make 6 dumplings. Partially cover and simmer 12 minutes or until dumplings are cooked through, spooning liquid from pot pie over dumplings once or twice during cooking.

Makes 6 servings

Savory Veg•All® Steak Pot Pie

- **1 pound beef round steak, cut into 1½ × ½-inch strips**
- **1 tablespoon olive oil**
- **2 cans (15 ounces each) VEG•ALL® Original Mixed Vegetables, drained**
- **1 can (14½ ounces) diced tomatoes, drained and liquid reserved**
- **¼ cup sliced ripe olives**
- **1 tablespoon cornstarch**

TOPPING

- **1 egg, beaten**
- **½ cup milk**
- **1 cup biscuit mix**
- **¼ cup grated Parmesan cheese**
- **1 tablespoon dried parsley**

1. Preheat oven to 400°F. In large skillet, cook beef strips in oil over medium heat. Stir in Veg•All, tomatoes, and olives. In small bowl, blend cornstarch with liquid from tomatoes. Add to skillet and cook for 2 to 3 minutes, stirring constantly, until mixture bubbles and thickens. Pour into greased 2-quart casserole.

2. To make topping: In medium mixing bowl, combine egg and milk. Add biscuit mix, cheese, and parsley; stir with fork until blended. Pour topping over vegetable mixture. Bake for 30 to 40 minutes or until heated through and crust is golden.

Makes 6 servings

Fried Buttermilk Chicken Fingers

CHICKEN

- 1½ **cups biscuit baking mix (regular, not low-fat)**
- 1 **cup buttermilk***
- 1 **egg, beaten**
- 12 **chicken tenders (about 1½ pounds total), rinsed and patted dry**
- ½ **cup canola or vegetable oil, divided**
-   **Salt and black pepper, to taste**

CREAMY MUSTARD DIPPING SAUCE

- ⅓ **cup mayonnaise**
- 1 **tablespoon honey**
- 1 **tablespoon prepared mustard**
- 1 **tablespoon packed dark brown sugar**

If you don't have buttermilk, substitute 1 tablespoon vinegar or lemon juice plus enough milk to equal 1 cup. Let stand 5 minutes.

1. Preheat oven to 200°F or "warm" setting. Place biscuit mix in pie pan or shallow dish. Combine buttermilk and egg in another shallow pan. Mix until well blended.

2. Roll chicken pieces in biscuit mix, one at a time, coating evenly on all sides; place on baking sheet. One at a time, dip each chicken piece in buttermilk mixture and roll in biscuit mix again to coat evenly; return to baking sheet.

3. Heat ¼ cup oil in large nonstick skillet over medium-high heat until hot. Place 6 chicken pieces in skillet. Reduce heat to medium; sprinkle lightly with salt and pepper, to taste. Cook 5 to 6 minutes on each side or until golden. Transfer to ovenproof plate. Sprinkle with salt and pepper again, if desired. Place in oven to keep warm. Heat remaining oil over medium-high heat and cook remaining chicken as directed above. Place in oven to keep warm until served.

4. For dipping sauce, combine mayonnaise, honey, mustard and brown sugar in small bowl. Serve with chicken.

Makes 4 servings

Texas Chili & Biscuits

1 pound ground beef
1 package (about 1¾ ounces) chili seasoning mix
1 can (16 ounces) whole kernel corn, drained
1 can (14½ ounces) whole tomatoes, undrained and cut up
½ cup water
¾ cup biscuit baking mix
⅔ cup cornmeal
⅔ cup milk
1⅓ cups *French's*® French Fried Onions, divided
½ cup (2 ounces) shredded Monterey Jack cheese

1. Preheat oven to 400°F. In medium skillet, brown beef; drain. Stir in chili seasoning, corn, tomatoes and water; bring to a boil. Reduce heat; simmer, uncovered, 10 minutes.

2. Meanwhile, in medium bowl, combine baking mix, cornmeal, milk and ⅔ cup French Fried Onions; beat vigorously 30 seconds. Pour beef mixture into 2-quart casserole. Spoon biscuit dough in mounds around edge of casserole.

3. Bake, uncovered, at 400°F for 15 minutes or until biscuits are light brown. Top biscuits with cheese and remaining ⅔ cup onions; bake, uncovered, 1 to 3 minutes or until onions are golden brown.

Makes 4 to 6 servings

Easy Salmon Pie

1	can (7½ ounces) salmon packed in water, drained and deboned
½	cup grated Parmesan cheese
¼	cup sliced green onions
1	jar (2 ounces) chopped pimientos, drained
½	cup low-fat (1%) cottage cheese
1	tablespoon lemon juice
1½	cups low-fat (1%) milk
¾	cup reduced-fat biscuit baking mix
2	whole eggs
2	egg whites or ¼ cup cholesterol-free egg substitute
¼	teaspoon salt
¼	teaspoon dried dill weed
¼	teaspoon paprika (optional)

1. Preheat oven to 375°F. Coat 9-inch deep-dish pie plate with nonstick cooking spray. Combine salmon, Parmesan cheese, onions and pimientos in prepared pie plate; set aside.

2. Combine cottage cheese and lemon juice in blender or food processor; blend until smooth. Add milk, biscuit mix, whole eggs, egg whites, salt and dill. Blend 15 seconds. Pour over salmon mixture in pie plate. Sprinkle with paprika, if desired.

3. Bake 35 to 40 minutes or until lightly golden and knife inserted halfway between center and edge comes out clean. Cool 5 minutes before serving.

Makes 8 servings

Mexican Skillet Tamale Casserole

FILLING

- **1 pound lean ground beef**
- **1 cup frozen corn kernels, thawed**
- **1 can (8 ounces) tomato sauce**
- **1 can (4 ounces) chopped green chiles**
- **½ cup water**
- **1 packet (1¼ ounces) taco seasoning mix**
- **½ teaspoon ground cumin**

CRUST

- **½ cup biscuit baking mix**
- **1 cup whole milk**
- **2 large eggs**
- **1½ cups (6 ounces) shredded Monterey Jack cheese or Mexican four-cheese blend**
- **Sour cream, sliced olives, chopped tomatoes, chopped cilantro (optional)**

1. Preheat oven to 400°F. Heat large nonstick ovenproof skillet over medium-high heat until hot. Add beef; cook and stir until browned. Drain and discard excess fat; return beef to skillet. Stir in corn, tomato sauce, chiles, water, seasoning mix and cumin; remove from heat. Smooth surface with spoon.

2. Combine biscuit mix, milk and eggs in small bowl. Stir until well blended; pour evenly over meat mixture. Bake 40 minutes or until crust is golden and knife inserted in center comes out clean.

3. Sprinkle evenly with cheese. Let stand 5 minutes before serving. Garnish as desired.

Makes 4 servings

Mild Green Chile Quiche

CRUST

¼	cup (½ stick) butter
1¼	cups biscuit baking mix
2	tablespoons boiling water

FILLING

1	teaspoon canola or vegetable oil
1½	cups chopped onions
2	cans (4 ounces each) chopped mild green chiles, drained
1½	cups (6 ounces) shredded sharp Cheddar cheese
4	large eggs, beaten
⅓	cup milk

1. Preheat oven to 400°F. Coat 9-inch deep-dish glass pie plate with nonstick cooking spray; set aside.

2. Melt butter in medium saucepan over medium-high heat. Remove from heat; add biscuit mix and water. Stir vigorously until soft dough forms. Cool slightly, then press dough evenly on bottom and up sides of prepared pie plate, forming rim; set aside.

3. Heat oil in medium saucepan over medium-high heat. Add onions; cook and stir 5 minutes or until translucent. Spread onions, chiles and cheese evenly over crust. Blend eggs and milk in small bowl; pour evenly over filling.

4. Bake 40 to 45 minutes or until knife inserted in center comes out clean. Let stand 10 minutes before serving.

Makes 6 servings

Hometown Deep-Dish Vegetable Pie

1	tablespoon butter
2	cups small broccoli florets (¾-inch pieces)
1½	cups sliced mushrooms
1	cup chopped red bell pepper
¾	cup finely chopped green onions
1¼	cups biscuit baking mix
¼	cup (½ stick) butter, softened
1½	tablespoons water
1	cup (4 ounces) shredded Swiss cheese
½	cup (2 ounces) shredded sharp Cheddar cheese
1½	cups whole milk
3	large eggs
½	teaspoon salt
⅛	teaspoon ground red pepper

1. Preheat oven to 375°F. Coat 9-inch deep-dish pie pan with nonstick cooking spray; set aside.

2. Heat medium nonstick skillet over medium heat until hot. Add 1 tablespoon butter. When melted, add broccoli, mushrooms and bell pepper. Cover and cook 2 minutes, stirring occasionally. Remove from heat, and stir in onions; set aside, uncovered.

3. Combine biscuit mix, ¼ cup butter and water in small bowl; stir to form soft dough. Shape into ball; flatten into disc. Place in prepared pie pan; press evenly on bottom and up sides of pan. Spoon vegetable mixture into crust; top with cheeses.

4. Combine milk, eggs, salt and red pepper in medium bowl; stir until well blended. Pour evenly over vegetable mixture.

5. Bake 40 minutes or until center is set and knife inserted in center comes out clean. Let stand 15 minutes before serving. (Do not skip standing step; crust will continue to cook and flavors will blend.)

Makes 6 servings

savory sides

Taco Boulders

- 2¼ **cups biscuit baking mix**
- 1 **cup (4 ounces) shredded taco cheese**
- 2 **tablespoons canned diced green chiles, drained**
- ⅔ **cup milk**
- 3 **tablespoons butter, melted**
- ¼ **teaspoon chili powder**
- ¼ **teaspoon garlic powder**

1. Preheat oven to 425°F. Line baking sheet with parchment paper or coat with nonstick cooking spray; set aside.

2. Combine biscuit mix, cheese and chiles in large bowl. Stir in milk just until moistened. Drop dough by rounded tablespoons in 12 mounds on prepared baking sheet. Bake 11 to 13 minutes or until golden brown.

3. Combine melted butter, chili powder and garlic powder in small bowl. Transfer biscuits to wire rack; immediately brush with butter mixture. Serve warm.

Makes 12 biscuits

Olive Herb Pull-Aparts

  1 **container (12 ounces) refrigerated flaky buttermilk biscuits (10 biscuits)**
     Olive oil nonstick cooking spray
2½   **tablespoons extra-virgin olive oil, divided**
  4 **cloves garlic, minced**
  ¼ **teaspoon red pepper flakes**
  1 **to 2 medium onions, very thinly sliced**
  ½ **(2.25-ounce) can sliced black olives, drained**
  ½ **cup shredded or chopped fresh basil**
  2 **teaspoons chopped fresh rosemary**
  1 **ounce feta cheese, crumbled**

1. Preheat oven to 400°F. Coat large nonstick baking sheet with nonstick cooking spray. Arrange biscuits on baking sheet about ½ inch apart.* Lightly coat with cooking spray; let stand 10 minutes.

2. Combine 1½ tablespoons oil and garlic in small bowl. Flatten biscuits. Sprinkle with pepper flakes, gently pressing into biscuits. Brush each with garlic oil, and top evenly with onions.

3. Combine olives, basil, rosemary and remaining 1 tablespoon oil. Spoon evenly over biscuits; sprinkle with feta.

4. Bake 10 minutes or until golden. Serve warm or at room temperature.

Makes 10 servings

For an attractive presentation, place 4 biscuits in a line down the center of the pan. Arrange the remaining biscuits, 3 on each side.

Chile Pecan Biscuits

- 3 **tablespoons cold unsalted butter, divided**
- 1 **large jalapeño pepper, cored, minced (2 tablespoons)**
- ⅓ **cup finely chopped pecans**
- 2 **teaspoons honey**
- 2 **cups biscuit baking mix**
- ⅛ **teaspoon chipotle chile powder**
- ¼ **teaspoon ground cumin**
- ½ **cup milk**
- 3½ **tablespoons shredded sharp Cheddar cheese (optional)**

1. Preheat oven to 425°F. Line baking sheet with parchment paper or coat with nonstick cooking spray; set aside.

2. Melt 1 tablespoon butter in small skillet. Add jalapeño and pecans. Cook and stir over medium heat 3 to 5 minutes or until jalapeño is tender and pecans are fragrant. Stir in honey; set aside.

3. Combine biscuit mix, chile powder and cumin in large bowl. Cut in remaining 2 tablespoons butter with pastry blender or two knives until mixture resembles small chunks. Stir in pecan mixture and milk; gently knead to form dough.

4. Turn dough out onto very lightly floured surface. Pat to ¾-inch thickness. Cut out biscuits with 2½-inch biscuit cutter, reworking dough as necessary. Arrange 1 inch apart on prepared baking sheet. If desired, pat about 1½ teaspoons cheese onto each biscuit.

5. Bake 15 to 17 minutes or until golden brown. Transfer to wire rack to cool.

Makes 7 to 8 biscuits

Antipasto Biscuit Sticks

- **2 cups biscuit baking mix**
- **½ teaspoon crushed dried oregano**
- **2 tablespoons cold unsalted butter, cut in thin slices**
- **½ to ⅔ cup milk**
- **¼ cup finely chopped pimiento-stuffed olives**
- **¼ cup finely chopped salami***
- **¼ cup finely chopped or shredded provolone cheese**

Hard salami is too chewy for these biscuits; use sandwich salami.

1. Preheat oven to 425°F. Line baking sheet with parchment paper or coat with nonstick cooking spray; set aside.

2. Combine biscuit mix and oregano in large bowl. Cut in butter with pastry blender or two knives until mixture resembles small chunks. Gradually stir in milk, adding enough to form a slightly sticky dough. Gently work in olives, salami and cheese.

3. Turn dough out onto very lightly floured surface. Pat into rectangle about ¾ inch thick. With sharp knife, cut into eight strips. Roll each strip gently into rounded breadstick shape. Arrange 1 inch apart on prepared baking sheet.

4. Bake 11 to 14 minutes or until golden brown. Transfer to wire rack to cool.

Makes 8 biscuit sticks

Yogurt Chive Biscuits

- **2 cups all-purpose flour**
- **1 tablespoon sugar**
- **2 teaspoons baking powder**
- **½ teaspoon baking soda**
- **½ teaspoon salt**
- **¼ teaspoon crushed dried oregano**
- **¼ cup (½ stick) cold unsalted butter, cut in thin slices**
- **⅔ cup Greek-style plain yogurt**
- **½ cup milk**
- **¼ cup sour cream**
- **½ cup finely chopped fresh chives**

1. Preheat oven to 400°F. Line baking sheet with parchment paper or coat with nonstick cooking spray; set aside.

2. Combine flour, sugar, baking powder, baking soda, salt and oregano in large bowl; stir well. Cut in butter with pastry blender or two knives until mixture resembles coarse crumbs. Add yogurt, milk and sour cream; stir gently to form soft sticky dough. Stir in chives. Drop dough by ¼ cupfuls 1½ inches apart onto prepared baking sheet.

3. Bake 15 to 16 minutes or until light golden brown. Transfer to wire rack to cool slightly. Serve hot or warm.

Makes 10 biscuits

Crispy Onion Flat Breads

2½	**cups biscuit baking mix**
2	**cups *French's*® French Fried Onions, divided**
1	**cup shredded Cheddar cheese**
¼	**cup grated Parmesan cheese**
½	**cup water**
2	**tablespoons *Frank's*® RedHot®** **Original Cayenne Pepper Sauce**
1	**egg white, beaten**

1. Combine baking mix, ⅔ cup French Fried Onions and cheeses in large bowl. Stir in water and **Frank's RedHot** Sauce until mixture is blended (dough will be sticky). With hands, knead dough until it comes together and forms a ball. Press into 6-inch square and divide into 24 equal pieces; cover with plastic wrap.

2. Move 2 oven racks to lowest positions. Preheat oven to 325°F. Crush remaining onions. Roll each piece of dough to ¹⁄₁₆-inch thickness on well-floured surface. Place on parchment-lined or ungreased baking sheets. Brush dough with egg white; sprinkle with about 1 tablespoon crushed onions. Prick dough with fork several times.

3. Bake 15 to 17 minutes or until golden, rotating baking sheets from top to bottom. Cool flat breads on baking sheets for 1 minute. Transfer to cooling rack; cool completely. Flat breads may be stored in airtight container for up to 1 week.

Makes 2 dozen flat breads

Sun-Dried Tomato Scones

  2 cups buttermilk baking mix
 ¼ cup (1 ounce) grated Parmesan cheese
1½ teaspoons dried basil
 ⅔ cup reduced-fat (2%) milk
 ½ cup chopped drained oil-packed sun-dried tomatoes
 ¼ cup chopped green onions

1. Preheat oven to 450°F. Lightly grease baking sheet; set aside.

2. Combine baking mix, cheese and basil in medium bowl. Stir in milk, tomatoes and onions. Mix just until dry ingredients are moistened. Drop by heaping teaspoonfuls onto prepared baking sheet.

3. Bake 8 to 10 minutes or until light golden brown. Transfer baking sheet to cooling rack; let stand 5 minutes. Remove scones; serve warm or at room temperature.

Makes 18 scones

Easy Cheesy Bacon Bread

- **1 pound sliced bacon, chopped**
- **1 large onion, chopped**
- **1 large green bell pepper, chopped**
- **½ teaspoon ground red pepper**
- **3 containers (7½ ounces each) refrigerated buttermilk biscuits**
- **2½ cups (10 ounces) shredded Cheddar cheese, divided**
- **½ cup (1 stick) butter, melted**

1. Preheat oven to 350°F. Coat nonstick bundt pan with nonstick cooking spray; set aside.

2. Cook bacon in large skillet over medium heat 3 to 4 minutes or until crisp. Transfer bacon with slotted spoon to paper towels. Reserve 1 tablespoon drippings in skillet, discarding remaining fat. Add onion, bell pepper and red pepper to skillet; cook and stir over medium-high heat 10 minutes or until tender. Cool.

3. Cut biscuits into quarters. Combine biscuit pieces, bacon, onion mixture, 2 cups cheese and melted butter in large bowl; mix gently. Loosely press mixture into prepared pan.

4. Bake 30 minutes or until golden brown. Cool 5 minutes in pan on wire rack. Invert onto serving platter and sprinkle with remaining ½ cup cheese. Serve warm.

Makes 12 servings

Bacon and Tomato Drop Biscuits

¼ **cup thinly sliced sun-dried tomatoes (not packed in oil)**

1 **cup biscuit baking mix**

1 **tablespoon cold unsalted butter, cut in thin slices**

6 **to 8 tablespoons milk**

1 **tablespoon minced fresh chives**

⅓ **cup cooked chopped bacon**

1. Preheat oven to 400°F. Line baking sheet with parchment paper or coat with nonstick cooking spray; set aside. Place tomatoes in heatproof bowl. Cover with very hot water; set aside 10 minutes. Drain well. Chop tomatoes to a pulp.

2. Place biscuit mix in medium bowl. Cut in butter with pastry blender or two knives until mixture resembles coarse crumbs. Add enough milk to make soft sticky dough. Gently knead in tomatoes, chives and bacon. Drop dough by heaping tablespoonfuls 2 inches apart onto prepared baking sheet.

3. Bake 14 to 16 minutes or until golden brown. Transfer to wire rack to cool slightly. Serve warm.

Makes 10 biscuits

Serving suggestion: Spread with cream cheese with chives for a great-tasting snack.

Tomato Cheese Bread

   1 can (14.5 ounces) CONTADINA® Recipe Ready Diced Tomatoes

   2 cups buttermilk baking mix

   2 teaspoons dried oregano leaves, crushed, divided

  ¾ cup (3 ounces) shredded Cheddar cheese

  ¾ cup (3 ounces) shredded Monterey Jack cheese

1. Drain tomatoes, reserving juice.

2. Combine baking mix, 1 teaspoon oregano and ⅔ cup reserved tomato juice in medium bowl.

3. Press dough evenly to edges of 11×7×2-inch greased baking dish. Sprinkle Cheddar cheese and remaining oregano over batter. Distribute tomato pieces evenly over cheese; sprinkle with Jack cheese.

4. Bake in preheated 375°F oven 25 minutes, or until edges are golden brown and cheese is bubbly. Cool 5 minutes before cutting into squares to serve.

Makes 12 servings

Corn and Sunflower Seed Biscuits

- **2 cups all-purpose flour**
- **4 teaspoons baking powder**
- **1 tablespoon sugar**
- **½ teaspoon salt**
- **½ teaspoon crushed dried thyme**
- **5 tablespoons cold unsalted butter, cut in thin slices**
- **1 cup milk**
- **1 cup whole-kernel corn***
- **⅓ cup plus 5 teaspoons salted roasted sunflower seeds, divided**

Use fresh or frozen corn kernels, thawed and/or drained. For best flavor, don't use supersweet corn varieties.

1. Preheat oven to 400°F. Line baking sheet with parchment paper or coat with nonstick cooking spray; set aside.

2. Combine flour, baking powder, sugar, salt and thyme in large bowl; stir well. Cut in butter with pastry blender or two knives until mixture resembles coarse crumbs. Add milk; stir gently to form soft sticky dough. Stir in corn and ⅓ cup sunflower seeds. Drop dough by ¼ cupfuls 1½ inches apart onto prepared baking sheet. Sprinkle ½ teaspoon sunflower seeds on each biscuit.

3. Bake 18 to 20 minutes or until biscuits are golden. Transfer to wire rack to cool slightly. Serve hot or warm.

Makes 10 biscuits

Light Meals

Hot Saucers

1 **container (12 ounces) refrigerated flaky buttermilk biscuits (10 biscuits)**
½ **cup finely chopped red bell pepper**
⅓ **cup diced ham**
2 **tablespoons mayonnaise**
1 **to 1½ tablespoons Dijon mustard**
¾ **cup (3 ounces) finely shredded sharp Cheddar cheese**

1. Preheat oven to 400°F. Coat large nonstick baking sheet with nonstick cooking spray. Split each biscuit in half for 20 rounds. Place in single layer on prepared baking sheet.

2. Combine bell pepper, ham, mayonnaise and mustard in medium bowl; mix well. Stir in cheese. Mound equal amounts in center of 10 rounds. Cover with remaining rounds, stretching gently to cover mixture completely. Press edges together to enclose filling.

3. Bake 11 to 12 minutes or until golden. Let stand 5 minutes before serving.

Makes 5 servings

Spicy Beef Turnovers

- ½ **pound lean ground beef or turkey**
- 2 **cloves garlic, minced**
- 2 **tablespoons soy sauce**
- 1 **tablespoon water**
- ½ **teaspoon cornstarch**
- 1 **teaspoon curry powder**
- ¼ **teaspoon Chinese five-spice powder***
- ¼ **teaspoon red pepper flakes**
- 2 **tablespoons minced green onion**
- 1 **container (7½ ounces) refrigerated biscuits (10 biscuits)**
- 1 **egg**
- 1 **tablespoon water**

Chinese five-spice powder is a blend of cinnamon, cloves, fennel seed, anise and Szechuan peppercorns, available in most supermarkets and at Asian grocery stores.

1. Preheat oven to 400°F. Coat baking sheet with nonstick cooking spray; set aside.

2. Cook beef and garlic in medium skillet over medium-high heat until beef is no longer pink, stirring to separate beef. Drain and discard excess fat.

3. Combine soy sauce, water and cornstarch in cup; stir until smooth. Add soy sauce mixture, curry powder, five-spice powder and pepper flakes to skillet. Cook and stir 30 seconds or until liquid is absorbed. Remove from heat; stir in onion.

4. Roll each biscuit into 4-inch rounds. Spoon heaping tablespoon filling into center of each biscuit. Fold in half, covering filling; press to seal tightly.

5. Place on prepared baking sheet. Beat egg with water in cup; brush lightly onto turnovers. Bake 9 to 10 minutes or until golden brown. Serve warm or at room temperature.

Makes 10 turnovers

Diggity Dog Biscuits

  3 **cups dry biscuit mix**

  1 **can (15 ounces) VEG·ALL® Original Mixed Vegetables, drained and mashed**

  ⅓ **cup whole milk**

  2 **hot dogs, chopped**

  ½ **cup shredded mild Cheddar cheese**

  ¼ **teaspoon garlic salt**

  1 **tablespoon chopped fresh parsley**

1. Preheat oven to 400°F.

2. Combine all ingredients in a large mixing bowl and stir until mixture forms a moist dough.

3. Drop about ⅓ cup of dough at a time onto a greased cookie sheet. Pat down lightly with the back of a spoon.

4. Bake for 10 to 15 minutes or until golden brown. Remove and let cool for 5 minutes. Serve.

Makes 12 biscuits

Serving suggestions: Serve with butter or ketchup.

Cheese-Topped Ham Biscuits

2 **cups biscuit baking mix**

½ **teaspoon crushed dried thyme**

2 **tablespoons cold unsalted butter, cut in thin slices**

⅔ **cup milk**

½ **cup finely chopped smoked ham***

¾ **cup shredded Gruyère cheese, divided**

2 **tablespoons melted butter**

1 **teaspoon Dijon-style mustard**

Substitute Canadian bacon, if desired.

1. Preheat oven to 425°F. Line baking sheet with parchment paper or coat with nonstick cooking spray; set aside.

2. Combine biscuit mix and thyme in large bowl. Cut in butter with pastry blender or two knives until mixture resembles small chunks. Gradually stir in milk, adding enough to form a slightly sticky dough. Gently work in ham and ¼ cup cheese.

3. Turn dough out onto very lightly floured surface. Pat to ¾-inch thickness. Cut out biscuits with 2½-inch biscuit cutter, reworking dough as necessary. Arrange 1 inch apart on prepared baking sheet.

4. Blend melted butter and mustard in small bowl. Brush over each biscuit. Pat 1 tablespoon remaining cheese onto each biscuit.

5. Bake 14 to 17 minutes or until golden brown. Transfer to wire rack to cool.

Makes 8 biscuits

Calzone-on-a-Stick

8 **wooden craft sticks**

8 **turkey or chicken sausage links (about 1½ pounds), cooked**

1 **package (16.3 ounces) refrigerated grand-size biscuits**

1 **jar (1 pound 10 ounces) RAGÚ® Old World Style® Pasta Sauce**

4 **mozzarella cheese sticks, halved lengthwise**

1. Preheat oven to 350°F. Insert craft stick halfway into each sausage; set aside.

2. Separate biscuits. On lightly floured surface, roll each biscuit into 7×4-inch oval. Place 2 tablespoons Pasta Sauce on long side of each oval. Top with sausage and ½ mozzarella stick. Fold dough over and pinch edges to seal. On greased baking sheet, arrange calzones seam-side down.

3. Bake 15 minutes or until golden. Serve with remaining Pasta Sauce, heated, for dipping.

Makes 8 servings

Peanutty Ham Turnovers

8   **ounces finely diced cooked ham (about 2 cups)**
1   **cup (4 ounces) shredded Monterey Jack cheese**
¼   **cup chopped roasted salted peanuts**
3   **tablespoons orange marmalade**
2   **tablespoons dried currants or raisins**
1   **to 1¼ teaspoons medium-hot chili powder**
1   **container (about 16 ounces) large reduced-fat refrigerated biscuits (8 biscuits)**

1. Preheat oven to 350°F. Line baking sheet with parchment paper or coat with nonstick cooking spray; set aside.

2. Combine ham, cheese, peanuts, marmalade, currants and chili powder in medium bowl; stir well.

3. Roll out each biscuit to 6-inch diameter on lightly floured surface. Divide filling evenly, spooning about ⅓ cup into center of each biscuit. Fold biscuits in half, covering filling; press to seal tightly. Place on prepared baking sheet.

4. Bake 15 minutes or until biscuits are golden brown and filling is heated through.

Makes 8 servings

Note: Refrigerate extra turnovers for 2 days or freeze up to 1 month. Place in individual resealable food storage bags for storage and packing.

Onion and Pepper Calzones

  1 teaspoon vegetable oil
½ **cup chopped onion**
½ **cup chopped green bell pepper**
¼ **teaspoon salt**
⅛ **teaspoon dried basil**
⅛ **teaspoon dried oregano**
⅛ **teaspoon black pepper**
  1 container (12 ounces) refrigerated biscuits (10 biscuits)
¼ **cup (1 ounce) shredded mozzarella cheese**
½ **cup prepared pasta or pizza sauce**
  2 tablespoons grated Parmesan cheese

1. Preheat oven to 400°F. Heat oil in medium nonstick skillet over medium heat. Add onion and bell pepper; cook 5 minutes or until tender, stirring occasionally. Remove from heat. Add salt, basil, oregano and black pepper; stir until blended. Set aside.

2. Flatten biscuits into 3½-inch circles (about ⅛ inch thick).

3. Stir mozzarella cheese into onion mixture. Spoon 1 teaspoon onion mixture onto each biscuit. Fold biscuits in half, covering filling; press to seal tightly. Place on ungreased baking sheet.

4. Bake 10 to 12 minutes or until golden brown. Meanwhile, place pasta sauce in small microwave-safe bowl. Cover with vented plastic wrap. Microwave on HIGH (100% power) 3 minutes or until sauce is heated through.

5. Spoon pasta sauce and Parmesan cheese evenly over each calzone. Serve immediately.

Makes 10 calzones

Corn Dogs

- **8 hot dogs**
- **8 wooden craft sticks**
- **1 package (about 16 ounces) refrigerated grand-size corn biscuits**
- **⅓ cup *French's*® Classic Yellow® Mustard**
- **8 slices American cheese, cut in half**

1. Preheat oven to 350°F. Insert 1 wooden craft stick halfway into each hot dog; set aside.

2. Separate biscuits. On floured board, press or roll each biscuit into a 7×4-inch oval. Spread 2 teaspoons mustard lengthwise down center of each biscuit. Top each with 2 pieces of cheese. Place hot dog in center of biscuit. Fold top of dough over end of hot dog. Fold sides towards center, enclosing hot dog. Pinch edges to seal tightly.

3. Place corn dogs, seam-side down, on greased baking sheet. Bake 20 to 25 minutes or until golden brown. Cool slightly before serving.

Makes 8 servings

Note: Corn dogs may be made without wooden craft sticks.

Baked Pork Buns

1 tablespoon vegetable oil

2 cups coarsely chopped bok choy

1 very small onion or large shallot, thinly sliced

1 container (18 ounces) refrigerated barbecue shredded pork

All-purpose flour

2 containers (10 ounces each) large refrigerated buttermilk biscuits (5 biscuits each)

1. Preheat oven to 350°F. Coat baking sheet with nonstick cooking spray; set aside.

2. Heat oil in large skillet over medium-high heat. Add bok choy and onion; cook and stir 8 to 10 minutes or until vegetables are tender. Remove from heat; stir in pork.

3. Lightly dust clean work surface with flour. Split each biscuit in half for 20 rounds. Roll each into 5-inch circle.

4. Spoon heaping tablespoon pork mixture onto one side of each circle. Fold in half, covering filling; press to seal tightly. Place on prepared baking sheet.

5. Bake 12 to 15 minutes or until golden brown. Serve warm.

Makes 20 buns

sweet treats

Chocolate Chip Cherry Biscuits

- **1 cup all-purpose flour**
- **3 tablespoons sugar**
- **¼ teaspoon salt**
- **2 teaspoons baking powder**
- **¼ cup (½ stick) cold unsalted butter, cut into thin slices**
- **½ cup half-and-half**
- **½ teaspoon vanilla**
- **¼ cup chopped sweet dried cherries**
- **¼ cup semisweet chocolate chips**

1. Preheat oven to 400°F. Line baking sheet with parchment paper or coat with nonstick cooking spray; set aside.

2. Combine flour, sugar, salt and baking powder in large bowl; stir well. Cut in butter with pastry blender or two knives until mixture resembles coarse crumbs. Combine half-and-half and vanilla. Add to flour mixture; stir gently to form soft sticky dough. Stir in cherries and chocolate chips. Drop dough by heaping tablespoonfuls onto prepared baking sheet.

3. Bake 8 minutes. Turn baking sheet around; continue baking 7 to 8 minutes or until biscuits are golden. (Bottoms should be rich brown, not dark.) Transfer biscuits to wire rack to cool slightly. Serve warm.

Makes 15 biscuits

Serving suggestion: For a delicious indulgent dessert, split the biscuits open and fill each with a small scoop of cherry-vanilla ice cream. Close the biscuits and drizzle lightly with chocolate sauce.

Decadent Brownie Pie

1 (9-inch) unbaked pie crust

1 cup (6 ounces) semisweet chocolate chips

¼ cup (½ stick) butter or margarine

1 (14-ounce) can EAGLE BRAND® Sweetened Condensed Milk (NOT evaporated milk)

½ cup biscuit baking mix

2 eggs

1 teaspoon vanilla extract

1 cup chopped nuts

Vanilla ice cream (optional)

1. Preheat oven to 375°F. Bake pie crust 10 minutes; remove from oven. Reduce oven temperature to 325°F.

2. In small saucepan over low heat, melt chocolate chips with butter.

3. In large bowl, beat chocolate mixture, EAGLE BRAND®, biscuit mix, eggs and vanilla until smooth. Stir in nuts. Pour into prepared pie crust.

4. Bake 40 to 45 minutes or until center is set. Cool at least 1 hour. Serve warm or at room temperature with ice cream (optional). Store leftovers covered in refrigerator.

Makes one (9-inch) pie

Peanut Butter Blossom Cookies

1 **(14-ounce) can EAGLE BRAND® Sweetened Condensed Milk (NOT evaporated milk)**

¾ **cup peanut butter**

2 **cups biscuit baking mix**

1 **teaspoon vanilla extract**

⅓ **cup sugar**

65 **solid milk chocolate candy pieces, unwrapped**

1. Preheat oven to 375°F. In large bowl, beat EAGLE BRAND® and peanut butter until smooth. Add biscuit mix and vanilla; mix well.

2. Shape into 1-inch balls. Roll in sugar. Place 2 inches apart on ungreased baking sheets.

3. Bake 6 to 8 minutes or until lightly browned around edges (do not overbake). Immediately press chocolate candy piece in center of each cookie. Cool. Store leftovers tightly covered at room temperature.

Makes about 5½ dozen cookies

Strawberry Cream Cheese Shortcake

- **2 cups biscuit baking mix**
- **2 tablespoons sugar**
- **½ cup (1 stick) butter or margarine, softened**
- **⅓ cup warm water**
- **1 (8-ounce) package cream cheese, softened**
- **1 (14-ounce) can EAGLE BRAND® Sweetened Condensed Milk (NOT evaporated milk)**
- **⅓ cup lemon juice**
- **1 teaspoon vanilla extract**
- **1 quart (about 1½ pounds) fresh strawberries, cleaned, hulled and sliced**
- **1 (13.5- or 16-ounce) package prepared strawberry glaze, chilled**
- **Whipped topping or whipped cream**

1. Preheat oven to 400°F.

2. In small bowl, combine biscuit mix and sugar. Add butter and water; beat until well blended.

3. Press on bottom of lightly greased 9-inch square baking pan. Bake 10 to 12 minutes or until toothpick inserted near center comes out clean. Cool.

4. In large bowl, beat cream cheese until fluffy. Gradually beat in EAGLE BRAND® until smooth. Stir in lemon juice and vanilla. Spread evenly over shortcake layer. Chill at least 3 hours or until set. Cut into squares.

5. In bowl, combine strawberries and glaze. Spoon over shortcake just before serving. Garnish with whipped topping. Store leftovers covered in refrigerator.

Makes one (9-inch) cake

Dutch Apple Dessert

  5 **medium apples, peeled, cored and sliced**
  1 **(14-ounce) can EAGLE BRAND® Sweetened Condensed Milk (NOT evaporated milk)**
  1 **teaspoon ground cinnamon**
  ½ **cup (1 stick) plus 2 tablespoons cold butter or margarine, divided**
  1½ **cups biscuit baking mix, divided**
  ½ **cup firmly packed brown sugar**
  ½ **cup chopped nuts**
  Vanilla ice cream (optional)

1. Preheat oven to 325°F. In medium bowl, combine apples, EAGLE BRAND® and cinnamon.

2. In large bowl, cut ½ cup (1 stick) butter into 1 cup biscuit mix until crumbly. Stir in apple mixture. Pour into greased 9-inch square baking pan.

3. In small bowl, combine remaining ½ cup biscuit mix and brown sugar. Cut in 2 tablespoons butter until crumbly; add nuts. Sprinkle evenly over apple mixture.

4. Bake 1 hour or until golden. Serve warm with ice cream (optional). Store leftovers covered in refrigerator.

Makes 6 to 8 servings

Hawaiian Bread

- ½ **cup sugar**
- ¼ **cup butter or margarine, softened**
- 2 **eggs**
- 1 **can (8 ounces) DOLE® Crushed Pineapple, undrained**
- ⅓ **cup chopped macadamia nuts or walnuts**
- 1 **cup flaked coconut, divided**
- 2 **cups prepared baking mix**

1. Preheat oven to 350°F.

2. Cream sugar and butter in large bowl. Add eggs, one at a time; beat well. Add undrained pineapple, nuts and ½ cup coconut and mix well. Stir in baking mix until just blended.

3. Pour batter into 9×5-inch loaf pan, sprayed with nonstick vegetable cooking spray. Sprinkle and lightly press remaining ½ cup coconut into top of cake.

4. Bake 50 minutes or until top is golden brown or toothpick inserted in center comes out clean.

5. Cool in pan 10 minutes; remove from pan and cool slightly on wire rack. Serve warm.

Makes 12 servings

Chocolate Pie

- ½   **cup reduced-fat biscuit baking mix**
- 3   **tablespoons unsweetened cocoa powder, sifted**
- 1¼ **cups sugar**
- 2   **tablespoons margarine, melted**
- 1   **whole egg**
- 3   **egg whites**
- 1½ **teaspoons vanilla**

1. Preheat oven to 350°F. Coat 9-inch pie pan with nonstick cooking spray; set aside.

2. Combine biscuit mix, cocoa and sugar in large bowl; mix well. Add margarine, egg, egg whites and vanilla; mix well. Pour into prepared pan.

3. Bake 40 minutes or until knife inserted in center comes out clean. Garnish with whipped cream and cocoa powder, if desired.

Makes 8 servings

Triple-Chocolate Pudding Cake

1   cup biscuit baking mix

½   cup sugar

¼   cup unsweetened cocoa powder

¾   cup milk, divided

⅓   cup butter, softened

¾   cup hot fudge topping, divided

1   teaspoon vanilla

1   cup semisweet chocolate chips, divided

¾   cup coffee or hot water

Fresh raspberries or whipped cream (optional)

1. Preheat oven to 350°F. Grease 8-inch square baking pan; set aside.

2. Combine biscuit mix, sugar and cocoa in medium bowl. Beat in ½ cup milk, butter, ¼ cup hot fudge topping and vanilla until well blended. Stir in ½ cup chocolate chips. Pour batter into prepared pan.

3. Combine remaining ¼ cup milk, ½ cup hot fudge topping and coffee in small bowl; stir until well blended. Pour over batter in pan. Do not stir. Sprinkle remaining ½ cup chocolate chips over top.

4. Bake 45 to 50 minutes or until set. Cool in pan 15 minutes on wire rack. Garnish with raspberries, if desired.

Makes 8 servings

Simple and Delicious Peach Cobbler

COBBLER

- **2** **cans (21 ounces each) peach pie filling**
- **½** **cup granulated sugar**
- **¾** **teaspoon WATKINS® Ground Cinnamon**
- **¼** **teaspoon WATKINS® Nutmeg**
- **1** **can (10 ounces) refrigerated flaky biscuit dough**
- **¼** **cup (½ stick) butter, melted**

VANILLA WHIPPED CREAM

- **1** **cup heavy whipping cream**
- **2** **to 4 tablespoons powdered sugar**
- **1** **teaspoon WATKINS® Vanilla**

1. For Cobbler, preheat oven to 400°F. Place peach pie filling in 13×9-inch baking dish. Combine granulated sugar, cinnamon and nutmeg in small bowl. Separate each biscuit into 2 sections. Dip each section into butter; roll in sugar mixture to coat. Arrange on top of peach layer. Bake for 20 to 25 minutes or until golden brown.

2. Meanwhile, prepare whipped cream. Chill small bowl and beaters of electric mixer. Beat cream in chilled bowl until it begins to thicken. Add powdered sugar and vanilla; beat until stiff peaks form. (Do not overbeat.) Serve cobbler warm with whipped cream.

Makes 10 servings

Shortcakes with Warm Apple-Cinnamon Topping

SHORTCAKES

- 1 **cup reduced-fat biscuit baking mix**
- 1 **tablespoon sugar, divided**
- 1 **teaspoon grated orange peel**
- 3 **to 4 tablespoons fat-free half-and-half**

TOPPING

- 1½ **teaspoons margarine**
- 3 **cups thinly sliced unpeeled apples, preferably Gala or Fuji**
- ¼ **teaspoon ground cinnamon**
- ½ **cup apple juice**
- 1 **teaspoon sugar**

Fat-free whipped topping (optional)

1. Preheat oven to 450°F. Line baking sheet with parchment paper or coat with nonstick cooking spray; set aside.

2. Combine biscuit mix, 2 teaspoons sugar and orange peel in medium bowl. Stir in half-and-half, 1 tablespoon at a time, until soft dough comes together. Gently knead 10 times. Turn dough out onto work surface. Cut into 2-inch circles with biscuit cutter, reworking extra dough to make 6 shortcakes. Place on prepared baking sheet; sprinkle with remaining 1 teaspoon sugar. Bake 12 to 15 minutes or until golden brown.

3. Melt margarine in large nonstick skillet. Add apple slices and cinnamon. Cook over medium heat 3 to 5 minutes or until apples are tender. Add juice and 1 teaspoon sugar. Increase heat to high. Cook 30 seconds or until juice is reduced by half and mixture is syrupy.

4. Split each biscuit in half. Spoon topping over bottoms; cover with tops. Add whipped topping, if desired. Serve immediately.

Makes 6 servings

Easy Lemon Pudding Cookies

- **1 cup biscuit baking mix**
- **1 package (4-serving size) JELL-O® Lemon Flavor Instant Pudding & Pie Filling**
- **½ teaspoon ground ginger (optional)**
- **1 egg, lightly beaten**
- **¼ cup vegetable oil**
- **Sugar**
- **3 squares BAKER'S® Premium White Baking Chocolate, melted**

1. Heat oven to 350°F.

2. Stir baking mix, pudding mix and ginger in medium bowl. Mix in egg and oil until well blended. (Mixture will be stiff.) With hands, roll cookie dough into 1-inch diameter balls. Place balls 2 inches apart on lightly greased cookie sheets. Dip flat-bottom glass into sugar. Press glass onto each dough ball and flatten into ¼-inch-thick cookie.

3. Bake 10 minutes or until edges are golden brown. Immediately remove from cookie sheets. Cool on wire racks. Drizzle cookies with melted white chocolate.

Makes about 20 cookies

Chocolate-Stuffed Doughnuts

- ½ **cup granulated or powdered sugar**
- ½ **cup semisweet chocolate chips**
- 2 **tablespoons whipping cream**
- 1 **container (7½ ounces) refrigerated buttermilk biscuits (10 biscuits)**
- ¾ **cup vegetable oil**

1. Place sugar in shallow dish; set aside. Combine chocolate chips and whipping cream in small microwave-safe bowl. Microwave on HIGH (100% power) 20 seconds; stir until smooth. Cover and refrigerate 1 hour or until solid.

2. Separate dough into individual biscuits. Scoop 1 rounded teaspoon chocolate mixture; place in center of each biscuit. Press dough around chocolate and pinch to form a ball. Roll pinched end on work surface to seal dough completely and flatten ball slightly.

3. Heat oil in small skillet until hot but not smoking. Fry doughnuts in small batches about 30 seconds per side or until golden brown on both sides. Drain on paper towels.

4. Roll warm doughnuts in sugar to coat. Serve warm or at room temperature. (Doughnuts are best within a few hours of frying.)

Makes 10 doughnuts

Shortcakes with Berries and Creamy Lemon Sauce

BERRIES

8 ounces frozen unsweetened mixed berries, thawed, including any juices

1 tablespoon sugar substitute

½ teaspoon vanilla

SAUCE

4 ounces sugar-free whipped topping

2 tablespoons sugar substitute

2 tablespoons lemon juice

2 tablespoons fat-free (skim) milk

SHORTCAKE

1½ cups biscuit baking mix

⅓ cup fat-free (skim) milk

2 tablespoons sugar substitute

½ teaspoon grated lemon peel

1. Preheat oven to 425°F. Coat nonstick baking sheet with nonstick cooking spray; set aside.

2. Combine berries with 1 tablespoon sugar substitute and vanilla in medium bowl; set aside. Combine sauce ingredients in separate medium bowl; mix well. Refrigerate.

3. Combine shortcake ingredients in separate medium bowl. Stir until just blended. Spoon batter onto prepared baking sheet in 6 equal mounds. Bake 10 minutes or until golden. Cool.

4. Split each biscuit in half. Spoon berries and sauce over bottom halves of shortcakes; cover with tops. Serve immediately.

Makes 6 servings

Shortcake Cobbler

- **2 cups pear slices**
- **2 cups frozen peach slices, partially thawed**
- **2 tablespoons raisins**
- **¼ cup water**
- **3 packets sugar substitute**
- **2 teaspoons cornstarch**
- **¼ teaspoon vanilla**
- **1 cup reduced-fat biscuit baking mix**
- **½ cup fat-free plain yogurt**
- **2 tablespoons granulated sugar**
- **2 tablespoons reduced-fat margarine, melted**
- **1 teaspoon grated orange peel**
- **¼ teaspoon ground cinnamon**

1. Preheat oven to 425°F. Coat 11×7-inch baking dish with nonstick cooking spray. Add pears, peaches and raisins; set aside.

2. Combine water, sugar substitute, cornstarch and vanilla in small bowl; stir until cornstarch dissolves. Pour over fruit mixture in baking dish; toss gently to coat.

3. Combine biscuit mix, yogurt, granulated sugar, margarine, orange peel and cinnamon in medium bowl; stir until well blended and mixture forms stiff batter. Spoon batter onto fruit mixture in 8 mounds. Bake 20 minutes or until topping is light brown. Serve warm or at room temperature.

Makes 8 servings